Our Walk
in the
Woods

by Charity Nebbe
illustrations by Jeffrey Ebbeler

mitten press

For Audrey, Carter, Rob, and all our canine friends.—C.N.

Text copyright © 2008 Charity Nebbe

Illustrations copyright © 2008 Jeffrey Ebbeler

All inquiries should be addressed to:

Mitten Press

An imprint of Ann Arbor Media Group LLC

2500 S. State Street

Ann Arbor, MI 48104

Printed and bound in China.

10   9   8   7   6   5   4   3   2   1

Library of Congress Cataloging-in-Publication Data

Nebbe, Charity.

A walk in the woods / by Charity Nebbe ; illustrations by Jeffrey Ebbeler.

p. cm.

Summary: As a young girl and her dog stroll through the woods at the beginning of spring,

they each have a very different perspective of their walk together.

ISBN-13: 978-1-58726-437-5 (hardcover : alk. paper)

ISBN-10: 1-58726-437-4 (hardcover : alk. paper)

[1. Spring--Fiction. 2. Dogs--Fiction. 3. Pets--Fiction.] I. Ebbeler, Jeffrey, ill. II. Title.

PZ7.N323Wal 2008

[E]--dc22

2007035276

Book and jacket design by Somberg Design

www.sombergdesign.com

This morning I got up very early.

This morning I got up very early.

We get up early every Saturday
because we like to take a long walk
in the woods.

I ate a quick breakfast and laced up my shoes.

Abby took forever to get ready this morning, even though I finished up the milk she left in her cereal bowl.

We love to explore the hills above the river.

This time of year is my favorite. The leaves on the trees are lush and green and all the flowers are beginning to bloom.

This time of year is my favorite. In the spring small animals are everywhere! Sometimes I get to chase them. Even if I don't see them I can learn a whole lot just smelling where they've been.

The place we walk is really beautiful, but this morning
I found a whole bunch of trash that someone had thrown
on the ground. That makes me so mad! I picked it up but
I had to fight Kirby for it.

Today was very exciting. When we got to the trail I found all kinds of great stuff just lying around on the ground. Abby wouldn't let me have very much of it, but I got some.

I like to take my time when I walk. I stop and smell the flowers, or look at the footprints that animals make in the mud. Even so, I still move a lot faster than Kirby.

The forest is my territory, but a lot of other dogs visit. I'm okay with that, but I do need to remind them just whose territory they are in. It can take a lot of time, but it is worth it.

Sometimes I
have to wait ...
and wait ...
and wait.

I'm great at digging. I'm better at digging holes than anyone else I know. I move through dirt pretty fast and when there's a tree root in my way I tear it out with my teeth. Like I said, I'm a fast digger.

One bad thing about springtime is that when the snow melts it can reveal some pretty gross things that have been hiding all winter. Kirby seems to find them all.

If I'm really lucky, I'll find something cool that has been hiding all winter under the snow. Sometimes it's something I can roll in to make myself smell wonderful. I don't know why but Abby gets really mad when I do that.

We love to run down hills. It makes us feel like we're flying.

My favorite spot on the river is a nice wide sandbar. I sit on a piece of driftwood while Kirby swims. I sit in the sun, feel the wind, and think about anything I want.

The best part of our walk is when
I get to go swimming. Sometimes
there are ducks and geese to chase.
Abby mostly likes to sit and watch
me. I'm not sure she knows how
to swim.

When I'm ready,
we head home.

We'll go again tomorrow.